The Waterhole

Archie's House

The Homestead

The Plane

Mitzi's

Ned's Caravan

The Windmill

Published by Ladybird Books Ltd
A Penguin Company
80 Strand, London WC2R 0RL
Penguin Books Australia Ltd., Camberwell, Victoria, Australia
Penguin Books (NZ) Ltd., Private Bag 102902, NSMC, Auckland, New Zealand

www.ladybird.co.uk

3 5 7 9 10 8 6 4 2

A Letter for George

Ladybird

In the outback, it's not easy being a postman – especially if you're a turtle, and a little slow.

George was running late as usual. He didn't like to just put the post in people's mail boxes. He preferred to deliver it in person. His favourite part of the day was saying "Good morning!" as he handed over the post.

"Hi, George!" called Frank and Buster as they saw him coming through the gate.

Just then, there was a furious flapping of flip-flops as Mitzi made her way over. "Hi, George," she said excitedly. "Have you got anything for me today?"

George searched in his satchel and
smiled. "I've got *three* letters for
you, Mitzi!"

"*Three!*" whooped Mitzi with joy.

As he handed Mitzi the letters, a
thought occurred to her. "I expect
you get lots of letters, don't you?"
she asked.

"Hmm," said George thoughtfully.
"No . . . not really."

Mitzi decided that *she* would write George a letter. Mitzi loved writing letters – long letters with lots and lots of lovely words in them. But the only trouble was, sometimes she wasn't sure what to say!

Mitzi shut her eyes and thought hard. 'Dear George,' she began. 'I like you because you're slow – no, that's rude. Umm, I like you because you bring me letters – no, he knows that . . .'

Eventually, she thought of just the thing to write!

'Dear George, you make me very happy because you bring letters from my friends, so I know what they're doing.
Love, Mitzi.'

11

The next morning, just as George
was emptying the post box in town,
he heard Mitzi calling him.

"Wait, George, wait!" she cried.
"I've got this for you!" She handed
George the letter. He stared at it
in amazement.

"For me?" he mouthed, stunned.

"Yes!" said Mitzi with pride. "I
wrote you a letter!"

"That's really nice," beamed George. "I'll read it later when I've finished delivering the post – so I can look forward to it!"

George carefully placed the envelope in his top pocket and patted it proudly. "I'll put it right here," he said. "Where it's safe." George was as pleased as could be.

13

Getting a letter from Mitzi put George in a really good mood for the rest of the day. He continued on his post round with an extra spring in his step.

"Look!" he said to Josie and Sammy in the General Store. "I got a letter from Mitzi this morning."

"That's nice," said Josie. "Are you going to open it?"

"Oh, not yet," said George with a twinkle in his eye. "I'm saving it for later."

Next stop on George's post round was the waterhole. He showed Alice and Archie his special letter too. They were very pleased for him. George smiled as he tucked the letter safely back in his top pocket and carried on with his rounds.

Now, sometimes a busy postman finds that with all the walking he does, his shoelace comes undone. And that's just what happened to George on the dusty outback road.

But, as he bent down to tie his shoelace, Mitzi's letter slipped from his top pocket, and fell onto the ground!

Later that day, when George had finished his rounds, he decided to sit down and read Mitzi's letter. He'd been looking forward to opening it all day. But where was it?

He searched every pocket, all through his satchel, under his hat, even inside his flask of tea! But it was no good.
    The letter wasn't there.

        Poor George. He was
            heartbroken.

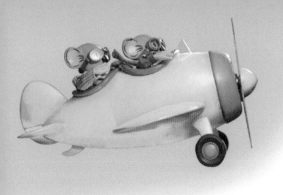

Meanwhile, the Koala Brothers
were out in their plane, looking for
anyone in need of help.

Suddenly, they spotted George!

"It's George!" shouted Buster.

"He looks a bit lost," replied Frank.

They landed the plane and went to see if George was all right.

"What's up, George?" asked Frank.

"Mitzi gave me a letter," said George sadly, "and I think I've lost it! I don't get many letters."

"Maybe you dropped it somewhere," Frank suggested helpfully.

Buster nodded. "Why not go back the way you came and search for it?"

George thought about this, and cheered up. "That's a good idea! Thank you!"

"Meanwhile," said Frank, "we'll fly around and see if we can spot your letter from the air!"

"Right. Yes. Thank you, Frank!" said George, smiling.

Frank and Buster took off again in the plane while George went back the way he had come with his head down, looking for his letter.

The search was on!

Over the outback, Buster squinted through his telescope at the landscape below.

"Do you see anything, Buster?" called Frank.

"Yes, lots," Buster shouted back. "Lots of *nothing*!"

But then, something *did* catch his eye. There seemed to be something small speeding along the dusty outback road. Buster blinked and looked again.

It was Alice, on her scooter! And in her hand she seemed to be holding something that looked very much like . . . a letter!

Excitedly, the Koala Brothers landed their plane again and went to find out what Alice had found.

"Look!" cried Alice. "I found a letter on the road! I think George must have dropped it!"

"Well done, Alice!" said Frank. "We've been looking for that everywhere.

"George will be really pleased you found it!" added Buster.

George was overjoyed to get his letter back. "Thank you!" he said happily. "I've been looking forward to reading Mitzi's letter all day!"

George put the letter safely in his satchel to read when he got home and set off, with a spring in his step, to finish his deliveries.

Frank began to wonder. If getting *one* letter made George so happy . . .

"I've got an idea," he announced. "Let's get *everyone* to write George a letter!"

"Yeah!" Buster and Alice shouted together.

And that's just what they did.

Everyone wrote a special letter for George. Even Ned, the little wombat, who wasn't very good at writing, drew a lovely picture with crayons.

The next morning, George went to the post box to collect the letters as usual. He gasped in amazement. There was *another* letter waiting for him! And another, and another! In fact, *all* the letters were for George!

At that moment, everyone tumbled out from behind the general store, laughing and cheering.

"Thank you, everyone," George beamed. "I'm so pleased, I don't know what to say."

"I'm glad you liked your letters," said Frank. "You know, if you *replied* to them all, you'd probably get loads more letters back!"

And that's just what George did. But it took him so long to write replies to all the letters, that the post was delivered even later than usual! But nobody seemed to mind.

And Frank and Buster both agreed that it's good to make your friends feel really wanted.

The General Store

Alice's House

Post Office

The Post Box